Dustin's BIG School Day

* *

WRITTEN BY **Alden R. Carter**

PHOTOGRAPHS BY **Dan Young and Carol S. Carter**

ALBERT WHITMAN & COMPANY * MORTON GROVE, ILLINOIS

Library of Congress Cataloging-in-Publication Data
Carter, Alden R.
Dustin's big school day / Alden R. Carter;
photographs by Dan Young and Carol S. Carter.
p.   cm.
Summary: Second-grader Dustin, who has Down
syndrome, anticipates the arrival of two very special guests
at his school one day.
ISBN 0-8075-1741-0
[1. Down syndrome—Fiction. 2. Schools—Fiction.
3. Puppets—Fiction. 4. Mentally handicapped—Fiction.]
I. Young, Dan, photographer, ill. II. Carter, Carol S., ill.
III. Title.
PZ7.C2426Du   1999
[E]—dc21   98-29567
                                CIP
                                AC

The design is by Pamela Kende.
The text typeface is Caslon.

About the Author and Photographers

Alden R. Carter is the author of thirty-one books for children and young adults, including the celebrated novels *Up Country, Dogwolf, Between a Rock and a Hard Place,* and *Bull Catcher.* With his daughter, Siri, he wrote *I'm Tougher Than Asthma!,* an *American Bookseller* "Pick of the Lists."

Dan Young is an award-winning photojournalist for the *Marshfield News Herald.* His work has appeared in the *Washington Post,* the *Milwaukee Journal, Current Science,* and numerous other newspapers and magazines, as well as internationally through the Associated Press. In 1995, he was awarded Best of Show by the Wisconsin News Photographers Association. His previous collaborations with Mr. Carter include *I'm Tougher Than Asthma!* and *Big Brother Dustin,* an Oppenheim Toy Portfolio Gold Seal Winner.

Carol S. Carter is a graduate of the Rocky Mountain School of Photography. Her work has appeared in several previous books by her husband, Alden. She served as photo coordinator for Dan Young on *Big Brother Dustin* and photographer on *Seeing Things My Way.*

For Sue Tormoen — A.R.C. & C.S.C.

For my parents — D.M.Y.

Many thanks to all who helped with *Dustin's Big School Day*, particularly John, Janet, Katie, and Steven Apfel; Dan, Judy, Chelsea, and Jacob Akin; Katherine Echola; Jamie Skjeveland; Robin Safford; Rae Fadrowski; Ann Gillett; Betty Juedes; Sally Hetzel; Greg Reierson; Joan Doak; Bev Shookman; Deb Mason and her students (especially Tony Sternweis and Lexi Morgan); and all the students and staff of Grant Elementary School, Marshfield, Wisconsin. Our families, our editor, Abby Levine, and the star of this book, Dustin Apfel, have our special gratitude.

Thanks also to Dave Parker and Skippy, who appear courtesy of Parker ProMedia Productions, P.O. Box 454, Marshfield, WI 54449.

oday is the day Dave and Skippy are coming to Dustin's school. "It's a big day, champ," his dad said as Dustin helped him tie his tie.

"It's the *biggest* day, Dad! Mom says so!" Dustin said.

Dustin's mom and his sister came with Dustin to the bus stop. "When are Dave and Skippy coming?" Dustin asked.

"At two," his mom said.

"I bet everybody loves Skippy!" Dustin said.

"Oh, I'm sure they will," his mom replied.

At school, Lexi, one of Dustin's best friends, asked him,
"How do you know Dave and Skippy?"
"Dave went to school with my dad," Dustin said.
"How about Skippy?" Lexi asked.
Dustin smiled. "I'm not sure. Maybe."

When the bell rang, it was hurry-hurry time to get coats and backpacks put away before class. Lots of people were talking about Dave and Skippy. Tony, who worried about things, said, "I hope they don't get lost."

"They won't," Dustin said. But he worried a little, too.

Mrs. Mason, Dustin's second-grade teacher, called the class to circle time. Lexi whispered to Dustin, "I wish Dave and Skippy were here right now."

Dustin only smiled and nodded, remembering that no one was supposed to talk out of turn in circle time.

"Lexi, if you're ready, we can start with the calendar," Mrs. Mason said.

"Okay," Lexi said. "I know the date."

Together they did the calendar, the weather, and sharing time. Everyone wanted to talk about Dave and Skippy.

Everybody had to be very quiet in the halls on the way
to music class. But in music, nobody had to be quiet because
Mr. Reierson always wanted *loud* singing to start a class.

"Louder!" he shouted. "I want Dave and Skippy to hear us
all the way downtown!"

After music, Dustin visited the speech therapist. Ms. Juedes helped him warm up with some lip-poppers in front of the mirror. "Say *Skippy picks pink and purple plums.*"

"Skippy picks pink and purple plums," Dustin said, popping every *P.*

"Very good. Now some tongue-lifters. Say *Dave's lion likes lemons and limes.*"

And Dustin did.

Next he worked on puzzles with Mrs. Hetzel, the
occupational therapist. "You were doing very well yesterday,
Dustin," Mrs. Hetzel said. "But today your mind is in the
clouds. What are you thinking about?"

"Dave and Skippy," Dustin said.

"Oh, that explains it," Mrs. Hetzel said.

In language arts, Mrs. Mason read the class a story about kites. Then they all wrote their own stories: *If I were a kite, I'd fly _____.*

Dustin wrote: "to see Dave and Skippy."

"All right, everyone," Mrs. Mason called. "Start making your kites!"

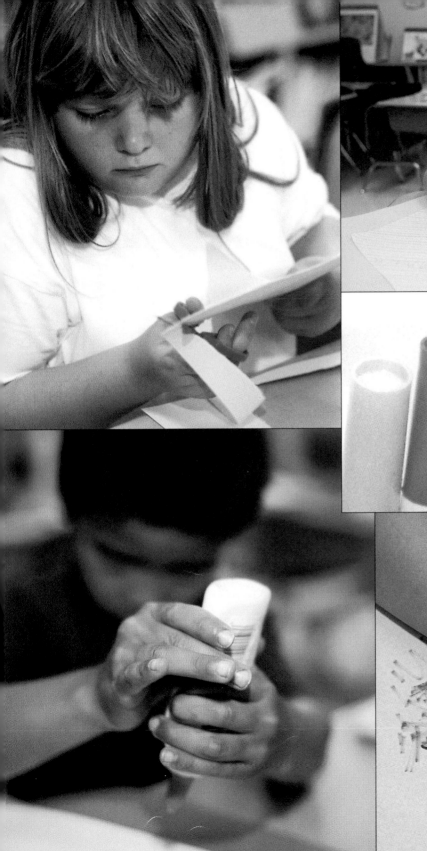

Outside it was bright and warm. Dustin, Lexi, and Tony scrambled over the jungle gym and then slid down the slide.

"What time are Dave and Skippy coming?" Lexi asked.

"My mom said at two," Dustin said.

"I hope they don't have car trouble," Tony said.

Lexi laughed. "Stop worrying!"

In the cafeteria, Dustin said, "I wonder what Skippy eats for lunch."

"Sawdust," Lexi said, and giggled.

"No," Dustin said. "Something lots better. Maybe pizza."

The class went to the library to find information on the animals of Africa. Dustin and Tony looked for Africa on the globe. Dave and Skippy traveled a lot, and Dustin wondered if they'd ever gone to Africa.

While the rest of the class did math, Dustin went to see Mrs. Fadrowski, who helped special kids with their reading and arithmetic. Dustin and his friends crowded into the bus they'd made.

"Let's do a math problem," Mrs. Fadrowski said. "If Dave and Skippy live four miles from school, and they drive two miles in the Dave and Skippy Express, how many miles do they still have to drive?"

"There's no room for them!" Gregory yelled.

"Yeah, it's too full!" Lizzie shouted.

Mrs. Fadrowski groaned. "All right, all right. Now watch my fingers. If Dave and Skippy live four miles from school and they *walk* two miles, how many miles do they still have to go?"

In science, Mrs. Mason showed them a wasp's nest.
"Termites also build nests," she began.
"I hope Skippy doesn't have termites," Tony interrupted.
Everybody laughed. "Well, it could happen," he said.
"I heard of lots of people getting head lice."
"Who's got head lice?" Mrs. Mason asked, looking just
a little pale.

After science, the class copied vocabulary words from the board and made up new sentences. Dustin had a folder with his own list of words to practice. Mrs. Fadrowski had added *Dave* and *Skippy* to the list. Dustin copied them in his very best printing.

The phone rang. Mrs. Mason picked it up. "Dustin, you're to go to the gym right away. A friend is waiting for you." Everybody cheered. Mrs. Mason hushed them. "The rest of you put away your work and line up at the door."

Dustin ran as fast as he could to the gym, completely forgetting the rule about not running in the halls.

"Hey, Dustin!" Dave Parker called.
"Hi, Dave!" Dustin yelled. "Where's Skippy?"

From a big black case came a rapping and a muffled voice.
"I'm in here! Let me out, Dustin! That crazy Dave locked me in again!"
"I guess we should let him out, Dustin," Dave said.

They opened the big black case. And, with a little help from Dave, Skippy sat up. "Well, it's about time! How do you expect a guy to breathe in there?"

"Say hello to Dustin, Skippy," Dave said.

"Hi, Dustin," Skippy said. "Ready to rock and roll?"

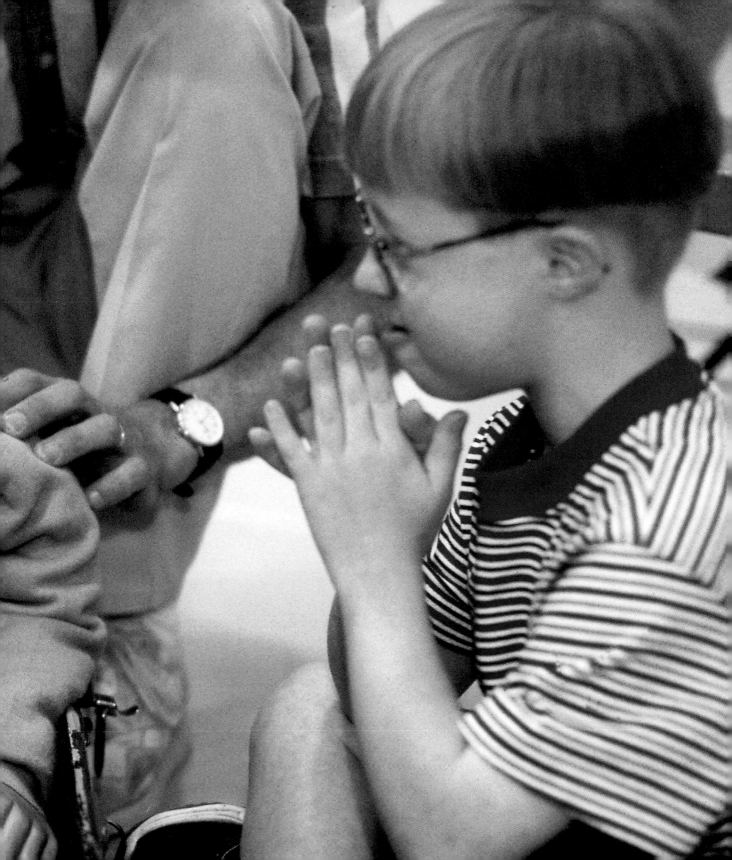

In a few minutes, the gym filled with kids. "What do you say, Skippy?" Dave asked. "Shall we make this first song for our friend Dustin?"

"Okay," Skippy said. "We'll sing, you play. That's if you remember how."

"I think I do," Dave said.

After the show, lots of kids asked for Dave and Skippy's autograph.

"It's been a big day, hasn't it, Dustin?" Dave said.

"The biggest," Dustin said.

Skippy yawned. "I'm sleepy," he said, and flopped like a puppet—which is what he was, of course—against Dustin's shoulder.